D1363911

JEFF ALLEN
VS.
THE TIME SUCK VAMPIRES

BY JUSTINA IRELAND
ILLUSTRATED BY TYLER CHAMPION

STONE ARCH BOOKS
a capstone imprint

THE LOYAL ORDER OF HELGA

Long, long ago, in a village called New Svalbard, the people who lived there faced unimaginable dangers. A sinkhole as old as time held a door – a portal – to the Otherside, a dark and dreadful place filled with literal nightmares.

To warn travelers of the danger the village posed, the people renamed it Devils' Pass – a reminder to all who lived there and passed through that a darkness sat in the area. A darkness that often had teeth.

For years the people of Devils' Pass endured the danger. Then Helga, one of the white settlers of the village, fell through the cursed sinkhole to the Otherside, coming face-to-face with the terrifying monsters. Helga spent many years there, fighting all sorts of monstrous creatures, learning about their ways and their weaknesses. Through trials and tribulations, and more than a little cunning, she became a fearsome warrior.

Helga fought her way back to Devils' Pass through the portal, now with an understanding of the deadly secrets of the Otherside. Almost immediately, her skills were put to the test. A fearsome frost giant menaced the village, crawling out of the sinkhole and terrorizing the people. Using only a flaming torch, Helga fought the giant and won. It was an astonishing act of bravery – but soon it was clear that the people of Devils' Pass suffered from something else. The sinkhole made the people of the village forget that monsters lived there.

Through some type of magic, however, not all of them forgot. Those who remembered the perils and nightmares the sinkhole brought forth became the Loyal Order of Helga. Along with Helga, the people who remembered the danger vowed to protect Devils' Pass – and the entire world – from the vicious monsters of the Otherside.

CHAPTER ONE
A Fight to Remember

Jeff sat in the waiting room at Devils' Pass Family Medical Center and tried not to feel nervous. It wasn't working. One of his worst memories of being in a waiting room had been the day the doctor had told him and his parents he had cancer, and it was a hard day to forget. His mother had cried and his dad had looked like he was going to throw up. Only his younger sister, Evie, had made him feel any better, patting his hand and whispering to him, "Science will help you beat this. Trust me. Science is the best."

Now, a year and a couple of operations later, Jeff felt nervous all over again. Not sick, like he had last time, woozy and nauseated. Just the kind of rabid nervousness that made his foot tap restlessly.

"Jeff, it's going to be fine," Ms. Allen said. She was a real estate agent, and she was still wearing her work blazer, a green jacket with the Allen Realty logo over her heart. She leafed through a magazine, but she was the only one. All the other people in the waiting room were playing on their cell phones. Jeff sighed.

"Do you think they'll take blood?" Jeff hated needles more than anything. After being poked continuously for two years straight, it hadn't gotten any better.

"It's just a checkup. I doubt it," his mom said.

"Can I borrow your phone?" Jeff asked.

"I left it in the car. It's really a distraction right now. I just downloaded that app your dad told me about, Hammer and Nail, and I can't seem to stop playing it." Ms. Allen laughed a little and then looked at Jeff

over the top of her magazine. "Have you thought about talking to your father about an advance on your allowance for a new phone, like we discussed?"

Jeff groaned. "Dad said he isn't buying me another phone until I can learn to be more responsible."

"Well, you have lost two phones in the past six months," Ms. Allen said, flipping the pages of her magazine.

"I didn't lose them! One got trampled by a doom unicorn and the other one was eaten by an elf of destruction."

Ms. Allen laughed. "That's hilarious! I love that you and your sister have such active imaginations. But now it's time to be serious, and your father is right. You've lost two cell phones. If you want another one you have to show us that you're responsible enough to take care of it."

Jeff crossed his arms and sat back in his chair. He was responsible enough for a cell phone. He and his friends spent their free time fighting the monsters in Devils' Pass as part of the Loyal Order of Helga. They'd fought killer mermaids and no-good brain toads — not to mention many other monsters that came from a place the Loyal Order of Helga only knew as the Otherside.

The problem was that most people in town immediately forgot the terrible things that happened right after they'd happened. Jeff's friend Tiffany called it "goldfish memory." So even though he really had lost his phone fighting doom unicorns and elves of destruction, his mom and dad would never believe him.

"Jeffrey Allen?" A pretty black nurse with braids had appeared in the doorway to the back of the office, and Jeff stood awkwardly. He usually liked to use his crutches, but his surgeon had said that to move on from his surgery, he had to wear his prosthesis more often. Since today's visit was all about reestablishing his care with his regular family doctor instead of the surgeon or oncologist, Jeff had reluctantly worn his new leg. It still felt strange to walk with it. Like wearing a too-tight shoe. It just didn't feel quite right.

Jeff followed the nurse to go see the doctor. Halfway down the hallway another nurse burst through a door, her pale skin flushed and her blond hair askew. "Where's Doctor Flinchbaugh? We've got another rage case!"

An older white lady sitting at a desk looked up from her paperwork. "Don't call it that! It's rude, Stacey. Say 'prolonged aggressive state.'"

No one acknowledged the older nurse.

The nurse escorting Jeff to the back frowned. "Another one? That's the third time this week."

The blond nurse nodded, and a woman in a white lab coat hurried down the hallway toward them. "Jane, did you say we have another rage case?"

"Yes, Doctor Flinchbaugh. A brother and a sister. Their mother said they'd begun fighting like she'd never seen before. They even tried to bite each other! Luckily, the mother and father were able to get them apart and drive them here separately. Every time they look at each other they start trying to hurt each other again. We had to sedate them when they came in, and they're still trying to kill each other."

"Let's get their blood drawn and do a panel to see if we can find out what is going on," the doctor said.

As the doctor and the nurse hurried down the hallway away from Jeff, he frowned. Rage case? That sounded serious.

"All right, let's hop on the scale here. Don't worry, I'll deduct some weight for the prosthesis," the nurse said with a wink.

Jeff flushed. As he stepped onto the scale a scream of rage echoed down the hallway. Jeff's eyes met the nurse's.

"I'm sure everything is just fine," she said.

Jeff wasn't so sure.

CHAPTER TWO
Just a Boring Block Game

Jeff got to school right as the lunch bell rang. The doctor had made him get blood drawn after all. He had also removed his prosthesis and poked at the spot where his foot had been attached to his knee after his rotationplasty, a serious surgery that they'd done to remove the cancer in his leg. During the surgery, the doctor had removed his knee and most of his shin, reattaching his ankle so that it now worked like a knee for his prosthetic.

The doctor's poking hadn't been for any real reason that Jeff could tell, since his surgeon was responsible for checking how the surgery had healed. Jeff hated feeling like something in a petri dish, and every visit to the doctor made him feel like he was less a patient and more an object of study.

So, being back in school? Well, it was better than being at the doctor.

He'd left his crutches at home since he already had his leg on, and a few people said things like "New leg, Jeff?" or "Whoa, they fixed your leg!" He forced a smile and said nothing, even though he wanted to point out that wearing the prosthetic was sometimes awkward and uncomfortable and there was nothing wrong with using crutches.

By the time he got to the lunch room and grabbed his tray, he was desperate for some time with the rest of the Loyal Order of Helga, his friends and the only people in town who seemed to understand him most days. The LOH was responsible for protecting Devils' Pass from the monsters that tried to eat the townspeople. The fact that they were kids didn't seem to matter. Jeff, his sister Evie, and their friends Tiffany Donovan and Zach Lopez kept the town mostly safe.

Tiffany and Zach were already at the table, laughing over something on Zach's phone. Jeff sat down and Tiffany looked up. "Hey! How was the doctor appointment?"

"Fine," Jeff said, poking his fork into what looked to be a pile of spaghetti.

"Cool," Zach said. "Is, uh, everything OK?"

That was always the question, wasn't it?

Jeff nodded. "Yeah, just routine to make sure everything is fine. Now that I'm no longer sick, I have to start going to my regular doctor again instead of the surgeon or the oncologist." No one said the word cancer.

"You're wearing your prosthetic again," Tiffany pointed out.

Jeff made a face. "That's a whole different visit. Prosthetics people want to make sure the fit is finally right. So I have to wear it all week." Jeff mostly liked his prosthetic leg; it let him move around a bit easier than his crutches. But sometimes it felt like a kind of reminder about his cancer, like the albatross around the sailor's neck in the poem they'd read in English class. He only had the prosthetic leg because of his cancer, after all.

And the last thing he wanted to think about was having cancer.

"Hey, have you seen Excalibur?" Zach asked, changing the subject. He did that a lot when Jeff talked about his leg. He tried not to let it bother him, even though it kind of did. This time he didn't say anything, because Zach was pointing at his phone screen.

"Excalibur? What is it, an app or something?" Jeff asked.

Zach got up and came around the table to show him. "Yeah. It's this game. See, the point is to uncover the magical sword. That's why it's called Excalibur. You know, from the sword in the whole King Arthur story and all? Anyway, you uncover these tiles and…"

Zach trailed off as he began playing the game while Jeff watched.

"Is that a new phone?" Jeff asked.

"Yeah, the Nosferatu 3. You can only use the app on Nosferatu phones." Zach trailed off as he started playing again.

A pang of jealousy shot through Jeff. His old phone had been a Nosferatu 2. It was a really cool phone.

Jeff looked over at Tiffany, who shrugged and said, "I don't get it, either."

"You don't have this game?" Jeff asked.

Tiffany shook her head. "Flip phone, remember? Mine doesn't have apps. But Evie downloaded it during PE. I saw her playing it in the locker room."

Zach was still playing the game, but Jeff couldn't figure out what was so cool about it. The game looked like just another boring block game.

Evie came running up to the table, her phone out and her tray precariously held in her one hand. "I just got to level three!"

"No way!" Zach said, looking up from his phone. "I've been stuck on level two all morning! Gah!"

Jeff looked across the table. Tiffany rolled her eyes and went back to eating her spaghetti surprise. Jeff tried eating his food, but he couldn't forget the nurses and their conversation.

"Hey, you look worried," Tiffany said, her mouth full of food.

Jeff nodded. "Yeah, when I was at the doctor's, the nurses were talking about something called rage case. Apparently a bunch of people have gotten angry and super aggressive."

"What do you think caused it?" Evie asked, not looking up from her phone.

"I don't know, and the nurses didn't, either. But it's been a while since we've had any Otherside monster problems, and I think we should probably check it out," Jeff said. If there was one thing he'd learned from being part of the Loyal Order of Helga, it was that almost everything tied back to monsters from the Otherside.

Devils' Pass was a nice town, but it was also a town beset by monsters. In the middle of the park was a sinkhole where the monsters passed through from the Otherside, a place only a handful of folks had traveled to and survived to tell about.

"So, does this mean a field trip to the sinkhole?" Evie asked, not looking up from her phone.

"Of course," Zach said, staring at his screen. "Maybe if something crossed over, it'll have left some kind of sign at the sinkhole."

"That's a good idea," Jeff said.

"We can take your new leg for a spin," Tiffany said.

"It's not new. Jeff just doesn't wear it," Evie chimed in.

"I thought you couldn't wear a prosthesis until everything from your surgery was completely healed?" Tiffany said.

Jeff nodded. "I got the prosthesis a couple of months ago. The doctor has just been adjusting it." Jeff didn't really want to talk about his prosthesis. He felt silly admitting that sometimes he felt mad or sad over even being sick in the first place. But these were his friends. If they didn't understand, no one would.

"Why?" Zach asked.

"It feels weird. It's just something else to get used to," Jeff said. He leaned over Zach's shoulder and watched again as he played Excalibur. Still boring. Why were he and Evie so into it?

"Hey," Tiffany said, distracting Jeff from watching Zach match colored blocks on his phone screen. "Did you ask your mom about getting a new phone?"

Jeff groaned and buried his fork in his spaghetti, taking a bite and swallowing it before answering. "It was a no go. She still thinks that because I lost my last two phones, I need to save up and buy a new one myself."

"But what about the elves?" Zach asked.

"And the doom unicorns?" Evie said, her tongue sticking out of the corner of her mouth as she tried to clear the level.

Jeff shook his head, and Tiffany gave him a sympathetic look. "Goldfish memory, huh?" she said.

"Yup. Neither of my parents remembers any of the monster attacks, or how they destroyed my phone, so I'm all out of options. I have to save up my allowance to buy a new one. And that's going to take forever." He let his fork drop back onto his tray.

Tiffany scraped the last of her spaghetti into her mouth and pushed her tray away. Evie and Zach had gotten lost in the screens of their phones, so she turned to Jeff. "Why not get a job? I just saw Mr. Ogilvie at the electronics store put a HELP WANTED sign in the window this morning."

"Don't you have to be like sixteen to work?" Jeff asked.

"You only have to be fourteen if you don't work a lot of hours. And since you just had that birthday, you could work with a permit," Tiffany said.

"That's not a bad idea," Jeff said, rubbing the back of his neck while he thought it over.

The bell rang, and Tiffany grabbed his tray to clear it along with hers. She froze, and frowned. "Hey, sorry, force of habit. I'm not used to seeing you walk around without your crutches. Did you want to get this yourself?"

"Nope, you can clean up after me." He forced a laugh and Tiffany rolled her eyes. Zach and Evie wandered off without a word, and Tiffany watched them go.

"Rude," she said, and Jeff had to agree.

He couldn't wait to get his own phone.

CHAPTER THREE
Will Work for Phone

After school Jeff, Tiffany, Zach, and Evie all headed down to the park. The park in Devils' Pass was nice, with a playground, trails where people could run or walk their dogs, and lots of trees.

And a sinkhole. The sinkhole was the bad part of the park.

The black water looked normal, if you didn't pay any attention to the rusty fence surrounding the property and the numerous NO TRESPASSING signs. But that black water hid the portal to the Otherside.

Only a handful of people had traveled to the Otherside and returned. Far more had fallen in, never to be seen again. The sinkhole was bad news, but the Loyal Order of Helga didn't have the luxury of avoiding it. Because the monsters it spawned had to be stopped. And they were the only ones who knew enough to stop them.

Jeff and his friends walked down the grassy slope to the sinkhole in silence. The grass was brown and crunchy, with a slight coating of frost. Jeff had to take his time when his foot slid a couple of times, since he was still a little unsteady on his new leg. A few dead leaves swirled ominously as a breeze picked them up, and Jeff shivered.

"I hate this place," Tiffany said, also shivering, and shrugging deeper into her jacket.

"Ditto," said Jeff.

Zach and Evie didn't say anything, but just kept looking at their phones.

Tiffany glanced at them and sighed. "Guess it's just

you and me," she said to Jeff.

The two of them walked the rest of the way to the sinkhole. The chain-link fence was rusty, and there were spaces where it sagged and bulged thanks to the horrors that came from the sinkhole. The fence had been patched many times, but there wasn't really anything that could keep the monsters from coming through. It was mostly just there to make people feel better about the unnervingly dark water.

"Doesn't look any different than last time we were here," Jeff said.

"I know," Tiffany said, walking around the fence. "Maybe the rage cases are really just some kind of medical emergency."

Jeff leveled a look at Tiffany. "When has anything in this town just been a normal thing?"

She sighed. "You're right. But there's nothing to worry about at this moment, anyway. If there's a monster in town, it'll show itself sooner or later. You should get over to It's Electric and see if you can get a job before they close."

Jeff nodded, and they made their way up from the sinkhole back to the path. Evie and Zach followed behind them, not looking up once. "What if Mr. Ogilvie doesn't want to hire me?" Jeff asked Tiffany.

"Well, my sister says if you're assertive, then you can do just about anything," she said. "Just don't take no for an answer. Point out how it would only be a few hours a week and that you're a super good helper. I'm sure you can convince him. After all, it isn't like there are a lot of people looking for jobs in Devils' Pass."

Jeff nodded. Tiffany was right. He would be confident and he would get the job at It's Electric.

He could definitely do this.

CHAPTER FOUR
It's Definitely Electric

Jeff said goodbye to his friends and headed down to Main Street and Mr. Ogilvie's shop. When Jeff was small, his dad used to take him there to buy radio-controlled cars and other odds and ends. Jeff hadn't been there in years, but when he walked into the store, everything looked exactly the same as it had when he was younger, all except for the wall of Nosferatu cell phones, their cases shiny and new.

"Never ever leave the phone in the sun! There are delicate electronics inside of the phone and if they overheat, the entire thing is ruined!" Mr. Ogilvie was behind the counter, talking to a high school girl with a broken cell phone. Mr. Ogilvie was an older white man with bushy gray eyebrows, glasses, and a permanent scowl. Every time Jeff saw him, he wore a sweater vest over a checkered shirt with corduroy pants. Today his sweater vest was green and his corduroys were blue.

"It was only in the sun for a minute, Mr. Ogilvie! I didn't think it could overheat so easily." The girl looked close to tears, and Mr. Ogilvie sighed.

"Well, your phone is still under warranty, so I can replace it for you for free. But you have to take care of these. Why don't you come back in an hour or so and I'll have a new phone set up for you."

"Thanks, Mr. Ogilvie!" The girl bounced out of the shop, the bells on the door ringing long after she'd left.

Mr. Ogilvie looked up from the broken phone. "Can I help you?" he asked, looking straight at Jeff.

"Hi, sir. You may not remember me, but I'm Jeffrey

Allen." He swallowed and tried to look confident..

"I know you. Your mom owns the real estate agency, right?" Mr. Ogilvie asked.

"Yes. I saw you were hiring, and I was wondering if maybe I could get apply for the job."

Mr. Ogilvie tapped his fingers on the counter and looked at Jeff. "You look young. How old are you?"

"Fourteen, but I can do whatever around the store. You don't even have to pay me. Well, not in real money. I just want a phone."

Mr. Ogilvie scowled. "Not paying employees is illegal. I like to keep things here on the up and up, young man."

The door opened and a tall, pale man wearing sunglasses walked in. He wore a suit and his dark hair was slicked back. He looked at Jeff and then back at Mr. Ogilvie. "Ogilvie. How are things? How are things selling?"

Mr. Ogilvie stood up straighter. "Vlad. Things are fine. The new line of Nosferatus is doing well."

Vlad nodded and looked over at Jeff. "Hello. Do you work here?"

"Yes," Jeff said. From the corner of his eye, he saw Mr. Ogilvie looking at him. Jeff stood up straighter and turned his full attention to the customer.

"I am Mr. Vlad, the Nosferatu dealer for this area. I have some boxes in the back of my car. Go get them and bring them into the store," the man said.

Mr. Ogilvie hadn't said anything, so Jeff went out to grab the boxes. Mr. Vlad's car was easy to find — it had the Nosferatu logo on the side of it and the trunk was open. Jeff grabbed the boxes out of the back, stacking them up and carrying them inside. It was awkward at first, because he felt a little unsteady on his leg, but after a moment, everything was fine.

So, maybe his prosthetic wasn't so bad, after all. It was heavier than he remembered his leg being, plus he felt really tired even after only a small bit of work. But wearing the prosthetic definitely had some advantages, he had to admit.

After he was finished, Mr. Ogilvie and Mr. Vlad shook hands and then Mr. Vlad left. Mr. Ogilvie looked at Jeff, a small smile on his face. "Well, you didn't work here, but I like initiative, so you work here now. Your hours are after school until six p.m. and on Saturdays from ten to five. I'll pay you ten dollars an hour, and you'll have an employee discount of fifteen percent when you're ready to buy a new phone."

Jeff grinned. "It's a deal."

"Great. Let me give you a tour of the store."

And just like that, Jeff was that much closer to a new phone.

CHAPTER FIVE

Hello? Are You Listening?

The next day at school, the Excalibur game was the only thing anyone could talk about. A few of the kids in Jeff's class, like Mason Briggs, had already gotten to level ten. A lot of kids, like Jeff's friend Zach, were still stuck on level eight.

"It's really hard because they add in this extra color. See? Light blue," Zach said. They were supposed to be working on a diagram of a frog's internal organs, but everyone was on their phones — even the teacher, Mr. Shin. Mr. Shin had given them all a lecture about not having cell phones in the class at the beginning of the year, and now he wasn't even mad when all the students were playing on their phones and not doing the assigned work. Weirder still, HE was playing on his phone. What teacher played a phone game during class?

Jeff looked over Zach's shoulder as he played, but he still didn't get the big deal about the game. It just looked boring.

"How many levels are there?" Jeff asked, labeling the frog's small intestine on his worksheet.

"Twenty, but apparently something amazing happens when you get to level twenty. I looked up the game on a message board on the Internet last night and everyone said level twenty is bananas!"

"Can I play for a second?" Jeff asked. Maybe if he played Excalibur, he'd figure out what was so special about it.

"Yeah, yeah, sure, right after this level," Zach said, staring intently at the screen. After a few minutes, it was clear that Zach wasn't going to let him play. It was like the game had a hold over him.

Jeff went back to labeling his frog diagram. Across the room Mason stood up and whooped. Everyone looked at him. "Level twelve!" he said.

"Twelve?" Mr. Shin said. "You were at ten at the beginning of class."

Everyone started talking, and a couple of people even walked over to check Mason's phone to make sure he wasn't lying. Jeff watched the whole scene, wondering what was going on.

"Does this seem strange to you?" Jeff asked Zach.

"What?" Zach asked without looking up from his screen.

"Everyone playing this game. Including Mr. Shin," Jeff said, watching as the class and teacher went back to playing their games.

"Huh? Did you say something?" Zach asked. He still hadn't looked up from his phone.

The bell rang and no one moved, as though no one

had heard it at all. Jeff packed up his things and made his way to the door. "Hey, the bell rang," he called when no one moved.

Folks looked up from their phones and slowly began to pack their stuff up. They shuffled out the door slowly, and Jeff let them pass as he waited for Zach.

"Uh, yeah. Great class everyone," Mr. Shin said halfheartedly, then went back to playing on his phone.

Jeff and Zach walked to the hallway. "I don't think that game's such a good idea," Jeff said. Zach was still playing as he walked.

"Hey, I got to level nine!" Zach showed Jeff the screen, where a tiny king holding a sword was jumping all over the screen.

Before he could bring up the weirdness of the game again, Zach moved off. Dread settled in Jeff's belly, heavy and cold.

There was definitely something wrong with that game.

CHAPTER SIX

Evie's Gone Mad

At lunch, Jeff told Tiffany about the way the people in his classes had been acting that morning.

"It's like no one even noticed the bell. That's weird, right?" he asked, taking a final bite of his lunch, then pushing the rest of the tray aside.

"Super weird," she said. Today was chicken nuggets and tater tots, and Tiffany had already finished hers. She had started in on the rest of Jeff's lunch by the time Evie and Zach showed up.

"Where have you guys been? Lunch is almost over," Jeff said.

"Oh, Evie was just beating level twelve! She was showing me how you have to watch out for the pink blocks, and then…" Zach trailed off as he looked back at his screen and started playing the game again.

"So you're at level thirteen. Wow! Evie, I think you're farther than anyone else," Tiffany said.

Evie didn't say anything, just kept playing the game.

Jeff and Tiffany exchanged a look, and Tiffany shrugged. "Hey, Evie, can I see your phone?"

Evie didn't seem to hear Tiffany, so Tiffany reached across the table and took the phone from her hands.

Evie froze, and Jeff felt a moment of fear. "Aww, hey, Tiffany, maybe that wasn't such a great idea…"

"YOU TOOK MY PHONE!" Evie screamed. She lunged across that table and swept Tiffany's lunch — really Jeff's lunch — right off the table and onto the floor. Tiffany's eyes widened, her face echoing the shock that Jeff felt.

Evie grabbed her phone and went back to playing, like nothing happened. Tiffany turned to Jeff.

"Yo. What just happened?" Tiffany asked, her eyes wide.

Jeff shook his head. "I don't know," he said. Evie was a pacifist. She never even defended herself against any of the monsters from the Otherside, let alone other people.

And yet, she'd decided to scream and throw things.

Just as weird, no one, not one teacher, came over to see what the commotion was about. Luckily, there was hardly any food left, so the floor was fairly clean. Jeff looked around and saw the lunchroom full of adults and kids staring at their phones.

The bell rang, and Tiffany grabbed her tray and Jeff's, which was still on the floor. Jeff followed Tiffany to the trash can.

"Are you OK?" he asked.

"Yeah, I'm fine. But I'm worried about Evie," she said, watching as Zach and Evie headed out of the cafeteria, their faces still bent over their phones. "That wasn't normal, and I'm starting to think maybe there's something up with that game."

Jeff didn't say anything. She was right. He'd had the same thoughts. What was it about the game that would turn his pacifist sister into a lunatic?

CHAPTER SEVEN
Rage Against the Night

Jeff went to work that night and then home, and nothing seemed out of the ordinary. Over dinner Jeff watched his sister carefully, and when Ms. Allen asked how their day had gone, Evie had only shrugged.

"It was fine," she said.

"You seemed upset at lunch," Jeff said, waiting for Evie to lose her temper again.

She only shrugged as she ate her baked tofu. "I just wanted to play my game. Everything's fine."

Whatever had made Evie act so strangely at school seemed to pass once she was at home, and he and his family ate dinner without incident.

The next day school passed uneventfully, and too soon it was lunch time all over again. Tiffany had a student council meeting at lunch and Evie had study group, so it was just Zach and Jeff at the lunch table. Zach didn't even bother opening his lunch bag, just spent all of lunch playing his game.

Jeff didn't say anything.

After school Jeff made his way to It's Electric, ready to work. The day before he'd only done a little stocking, setting up the new Nosferatu phones along the wall and dusting off the ones that were already there. It's Electric didn't just sell cell phones. The store also had a few radio-controlled cars and battery displays, but it was pretty clear that the biggest draw was the cell phones. People were always stopping in to pick up the phones and look at them. The phones were really expensive, so not everyone bought one. But it was obvious everyone wanted one.

"It's about time you got here," Mr. Ogilvie said when Jeff got to the store. "Vlad dropped off some more phones this morning. The boxes need to be stocked up in the back." Jeff wasn't late — he was actually fifteen minutes early. But Mr. Ogilvie had a way of making it sound like Jeff had done something wrong even when giving praise.

Jeff set down his backpack and made his way to the back room.

There were a ton of boxes and stuff kicked around, and Jeff spent most of the evening stacking up the boxes and wondering how it had gotten to be such a mess. By the time he'd cleaned up the chaos in the store room, he was ready to go home. The leg he wore his prosthetic on had begun to ache. Mr. Ogilvie was always happy to let him go home once he'd finished all of his tasks for the day. Jeff's physical therapist had told him wearing his leg would be an adjustment process, but Jeff still felt impatient at how sometimes the leg worked great and sometimes it made things awkward. His mom called it growing pains. Jeff called it annoying.

Mr. Ogilvie was with a customer when Jeff came out of the stock room, so he stood back a little and waited. When the woman walked off to look at the cell phones, Jeff walked up to Mr. Ogilvie.

"I straightened up the stock room. I'm going to head home now since everything is done. And it's almost six anyway," he said.

"Fine, fine," Mr. Ogilvie said, waving his hand at Jeff. "See you tomorrow."

Jeff let himself out and started to walk home. It was cold out and already dark, and even though he wasn't really afraid of the dark, it was freaky to be out and about by himself.

It was Devils' Pass, after all.

Jeff took a shortcut down a side street and saw someone in the middle of the road. The person was just standing there, not crossing the street, just blocking the lane. Even though there was no traffic, it seemed strange to see someone standing in the middle of the road like that.

"Hey, are you OK?" Jeff called. The person turned around and growled. Jeff took a stumbling step back.

It was Mason Briggs. Mason's hair stuck up in every direction and his lips were pulled back from his teeth in a snarl. He took a few steps toward Jeff. Mason's steps were heavy and his fists were clenched.

"Mason, what's going on?" Jeff asked, taking another step back.

Mason didn't say anything, just began running at Jeff. He snarled, and Jeff did the only sensible thing.

He ran.

Running with his prosthesis wasn't like running with his leg had been, and it took him a few steps to get the rhythm of it down. But once he did, he didn't bother looking back to see if Mason was chasing him. Mason screamed as he ran, huffing and growling and acting completely out of control.

This, thought Jeff, was what the nurse must have been talking about.

Mason had gone full-on rage case.

Jeff turned the corner and ran across the street without looking. A bright light coming down the road

startled him, and it took a moment for Jeff to realize that it was a car, going much too fast. His fear dropped away and panic sent ice through his veins. There was nothing he could do but keep running.

He waited for the impact, for the car to hit him, but it didn't.

Tires squealed and the car swerved to miss him. It was quickly followed by a thump as the car hit Mason instead, sending him up over the hood and then onto the ground.

Jeff ran toward Mason but tripped over his feet and fell. It took him a moment to get himself sorted out and to climb to his feet. When he did, there was his neighbor, Mr. Charles, on the phone, looking down at Mason lying prone on the ground.

"Are you OK?" Mr. Charles asked Jeff.

"Yes," Jeff said, making his way over to Mason. Jeff had to see if Mason was OK.

Mason lay on his back but didn't say anything. Just stared into space, drool leaking out of the corner of his mouth. Every so often he would blink, slowly. He wasn't angry anymore, and he didn't even seem to be hurt.

The sound of sirens echoed down the street, and Jeff climbed to his feet. He had to talk to the rest of the Loyal Order of Helga about this. Because Mason definitely wasn't the kind of guy to chase someone down the street. Something was very, very wrong.

There had to be monsters in town.

CHAPTER EIGHT
No Games, Please

By the time Jeff had gotten home after Mason's accident, it had been too late to call any of his friends. So he shot off an email to everyone trying to explain what had happened. Then he spent a restless night trying to sleep until finally it was time to go to school.

Jeff found Tiffany standing next to her locker and reading a book when he walked in. She took a bite of an apple and looked up when he approached.

"Nice to see you haven't fallen under the spell of Excalibur," Tiffany said, swallowing the bite. She waved her hand to indicate everyone else in the hallway, their faces bent close to their phones as they played the game.

"No phone, remember?" Jeff said, pointing to himself. "But I'm starting to think it might be a good thing."

"No doubt. My flip phone is looking really good about now," Tiffany said, tossing her apple core into a nearby trash can. "I saw your email this morning. So, you think Excalibur is making people rage?"

Jeff nodded. "Definitely. Mason was further in the game than anyone else."

Tiffany nodded. "OK, so what exactly happened last night? I want to hear it again."

Jeff outlined what had happened the night before, and Tiffany slowly closed her book and put it away in her locker.

"Jeff, that's serious. Are you sure Excalibur is causing this stuff?"

"I don't know. I do know that Zach told me

yesterday that when folks got to level twenty, something special happened. What if there's something in the game that makes people rage?"

"What are you saying? You think monsters from the Otherside designed the Excalibur app?" She furrowed her brow.

Jeff nodded. "Yeah. It makes perfect sense. The whole town of Devils' Pass seems obsessed with the game. Why not monsters?"

"OK, but what kind of monster could do that? I mean, most of the monsters we deal with are trying to eat folks, not make them kill each other," she said.

Jeff shrugged. "I don't know. I mean, anyone can develop an app. Remember when Adrian Freeland developed that app to track the melting times of the different flavors of JELL-O in the cafeteria?"

Tiffany tapped her finger against her lips. "OK, so let's say that monsters did develop the app. What's their plan? Make everyone play and then take over the town once they're angry? That seems like the opposite of how they'd want folks to behave."

Jeff sighed. "I don't know. None of it makes sense."

The warning bell rang, and Tiffany fluffed her Afro puff. "Look, this game is obviously bad news. We need to talk to Mr. Hofstrom. No one knows monsters like he does."

Mr. Hofstrom had once fallen through the sinkhole to the Otherside. He'd been there nearly twenty years, even though when he came back to the regular world, he hadn't aged a day. He knew more about monsters than anyone else. If there was a monster that could develop an app, Mr. Hofstrom would know what it was.

"I have work right after school, but I'm done at six. We could go over there then," Jeff said.

"Good idea. We should probably get Evie and Zach to come to the library with us. Both of them are totally addicted to the game, and Mr. Hofstrom might be able to help them before it gets even more serious." Tiffany shut her locker.

Jeff nodded. "Sounds good. See you at lunch."

"You too. Oh, and Jeff?"

"Yeah?"

"Don't play the game, no matter how much you might want to. The last thing we need is everyone in town addicted to it." She waved at him and then headed down the hallway to her class.

Jeff nodded, and made his way to his first class of the day, but a tendril of worry began to gnaw at the back of his mind.

What if the app wasn't the thing causing the rage cases? What then?

CHAPTER NINE

Another One Down

Everyone was playing Excalibur. Even the few kids that never played games on their phone. Every class Jeff went to, it seemed like he and a couple of other kids were the only ones paying attention, the only ones without phones. He was jealous and relieved at the same time, and it was a strange feeling.

He walked to lunch slowly, his prosthesis bothering him. He missed his crutches.

His prosthetic leg wasn't painful, it was just
uncomfortable, like wearing a too-tight sock on
his foot. He mostly tried not to think about his
prosthetic leg, but today the tug and pull of it was a
distraction from the fact that almost the entire school
was playing Excalibur.

How many of them would become rage cases?

Tiffany was the only one of his friends at lunch,
Zach and Evie not even coming to eat. Halfway
through lunch, Tiffany patted his hand. "We'll figure
this out. Mr. Hofstrom will have the answers." Jeff
realized that he should be doing something about
Evie — like taking her phone away or something else
— but he couldn't bring himself to. She'd gotten so
angry.

He was also worried that he was wrong. Mason
had already gone rage case, and it was anyone's
guess who would be next. If it was the app causing
the change in people, then that meant Evie was
in danger. But if it wasn't the app then they were
wasting time chasing down the wrong path and that

meant more people could get hurt like Mason. Or even worse.

But if the app wasn't causing the rage cases what was? The whole situation made his head hurt.

"Jeff!" Tiffany said, startling him.

"Oh, sorry, what?"

"I asked you how many rage cases the doctor's office had seen? Did the nurses say?" She crossed her arms and waited for his answer.

Jeff shook his head. "No. I didn't hear."

"I had a study period for English today and I found out that Excalibur has been out since last summer. So, if that's what's causing folks to become rage-y, it seems strange that it would take effect all of a sudden," Tiffany said.

A tray crashed to the floor, and Tiffany and Jeff turned toward the lunch line. Standing in the line was Nellie Ayers. Nellie was the kind of girl who always downloaded every app and video game before anyone else had heard of it. Now, Nellie's skin was pale and waxy and she was staring at the lunch lady, growling.

Nellie picked up another lunch tray and threw it across the room. People shouted and ducked.

"I SAID I WANT MACARONI AND CHEESE!" Nellie screamed. She tried to climb the sneeze guard that separated students from the lunch line. The lunch ladies behind the line backpedaled and the cafeteria monitors ran over to subdue Nellie. It took a teacher on each arm and one holding her feet to carry her out of the cafeteria, Nellie screaming the entire time.

"Oh. Wow," Tiffany said. "You weren't joking about the rage."

Jeff nodded. "Another one bites the dust."

"Grim," Tiffany said. "I'm going to sneak out and call the hospital. I'll see if I can get any information on what happens to the people who go rage-y. See you later tonight." Tiffany grabbed her tray and left.

Jeff watched as the teachers talked to the lunch ladies, trying to calm them down after the

confrontation. But he was only half paying attention to them.

He had to find out if the app was causing this before Evie's mind completely gave in to rage.

He just couldn't let that happen.

CHAPTER TEN

The App's the Thing. Right?

Jeff moved through his shift at It's Electric in a daze, his mind focused on Excalibur and the people who had gone rage case, not on the conversation between Mr. Ogilvie and Mr. Vlad. They stood in the back office talking about the new phones and plans for a launch, and it wasn't until Mr. Ogilvie called Jeff back that he realized he should have been listening in.

"Jeff, Mr. Vlad and I had an idea about the launch on Saturday and we need your help," Mr. Ogilvie said, stopping Jeff before he could leave at the end of his shift.

"Oh, OK."

Mr. Vlad rubbed his chin and smiled down at Jeff in a way that gave him the creeps. "Nosferatu has partnered with the makers of Excalibur to launch the new line of phones. All of our devices will now come preloaded with Excalibur."

"Excalibur?" Jeff said, taking a slight step back.

"Yes! Have you heard of it? It's very popular. Anyway, we're doing the official launch here at It's Electric this Saturday, and we thought it might be great to have you dress up as a king," Mr. Vlad finished, still smiling. Jeff looked up at him, but all he saw was his own pale face reflected back in the lenses of the sunglasses.

"You want me to dress up as a king," Jeff said, echoing Mr. Vlad.

"Yes. Apparently the character in the game is a tiny little king or some nonsense," Mr. Ogilvie said, taking off his glasses and rubbing the lenses.

"I don't think me dressing up is a good idea," Jeff said.

Mr. Vlad and Mr. Ogilvie exchanged a look. Mr. Vlad smiled. "Embarrassed, are we?"

"No, I just don't' think I, um, would be good at it," Jeff said. He couldn't very well tell him that he was too busy trying to figure out if their app was making people turn into raging bullies. He didn't even know if it was the app that caused the rage cases, yet.

"How about if I pay you double on Saturday?" Mr. Ogilvie said.

"Double?" Jeff asked.

"Yep. You'll be able to get your very own Nosferatu by the end of the day," Mr. Ogilvie said with a smile.

Mr. Ogilvie never smiled.

"OK," Jeff said. "I'll dress up as the king from Excalibur."

"Excellent!" Mr. Vlad said, clapping his hands. "I'm willing to bet that this will be a launch to remember."

Jeff nodded.

But if it turned out that Excalibur was causing the rage cases, Jeff would make sure there wasn't a launch at all.

CHAPTER ELEVEN

Getting Reflective

Jeff arrived at the library just as Mr. Hofstrom was locking the doors. "Just in time, man. The rest of your people are inside already," Mr. Hofstrom said.

The mayor of Devils' Pass had given Mr. Hofstrom a job at the library and made him the unofficial keeper of history. Like the Loyal Order of Helga and the mayor (most of the time), Mr. Hofstrom didn't suffer from goldfish memory.

Mr. Hofstrom was definitely the coolest adult that Jeff knew. He always wore jogging pants and a T-shirt with a light windbreaker over the top. He looked like he was more likely to go for a jog than talk about books. But he also knew just about everything there was to know about the sinkhole, and that knowledge was invaluable to the Loyal Order of Helga.

Jeff followed Mr. Hofstrom into the library. Zach and Evie were at the table in the middle of the reading area, both of them inches away from their phones. Tiffany paced around the outside of the table, a scowl on her face.

Jeff walked over to Tiffany while Mr. Hofstrom finished locking the main doors.

"Hey, was it hard to get Evie and Zach here?" he asked.

She shrugged. "Oh, it was fine. They have no idea where they are right now. Nothing matters as long as they have the game."

Jeff looked at Zach and Evie. He could no longer hold back the worry he'd been fighting all day. "This is bad," he said.

"Oh, most definitely. But the bright side is that this isn't unfixable," Mr. Hofstrom said, calm as usual.

"How do we fix it?" Jeff asked.

Mr. Hofstrom shrugged. "You just have to kill the queen."

"What?" Jeff asked.

"Mr. Hofstrom thinks it might be vampires," Tiffany said.

"Vampires?" Jeff said, sinking into a chair across from Evie. Her eyes were glued to the screen, and she didn't even register Jeff's presence.

"Vampires," said Mr. Hofstrom as he walked up. "If your app is making everyone go 'rage case' as Tiffany called it, it's most definitely caused by vampires."

"But I thought vampires drink blood and hypnotize people," Jeff said. "This seems like a really weird way to get blood."

"Vampires are about sucking up energy," Mr. Hofstrom said, taking the chair at the head of the table. "How they manage to do that is less important than actually stealing the energy. Some vampires drink blood, some steal dreams, and whatever vampire designed this computer game is stealing people's energy by making them focus on playing the game until their mind is obsessed and they're consumed with rage. Nothing generates more energy than rage. Have you ever heard of Limit-Based Neuron Overload? Most people call it a 'rage quit'?"

Jeff frowned. "Basically when people get angry and quit a game because it's too hard to play?"

Mr. Hofstrom nodded. "Exactly. Vampires were responsible for some of those games. There was nothing tastier to them than a good rage quit. These vampires, however, seem to be a little different. People are going all the way to the end of the game. These vampires appear to be a lot greedier than other ones I've run into. I've never heard of anything like the rage cases Tiffany told me about. That must be a bigger energy burst than a simple rage quit. And most likely that burst of energy requires the player to be emotionally invested in the game, hence the rumors about something amazing happening when you beat level twenty."

Tiffany nodded slowly. "I could see that. If I'm not emotionally invested in something, it's not as big a deal to quit. But if I'm really looking forward to something, that frustration will be a whole lot bigger."

Mr. Hofstrom's lips thinned. And the result is emotional overload. Rage case, as you called it."

"How do we stop them?" Jeff asked.

"Well, vampires work like a beehive, with a queen ruling them all. If you can defeat the queen, you can help all of your friends."

"Remember when Zach was saying something about making it to level twenty or so?" Tiffany said.

Jeff shrugged. "Yeah. Why?"

"I went over to Mason's house and talked to his sister. Betsy is friends with my sister. Anyway, he was apparently telling his sister at dinner how he was on level nineteen and he was going to beat the game before anyone else at school," Tiffany said.

Jeff buried his head in his hands. "You think he made it to level twenty and then can't beat it so, bloop, rage case?"

"Yep. I tried calling the hospital about their rage cases, but they wouldn't tell me about anybody specific. But the nurse did say that they'd had twenty people admitted since last week."

"Twenty! That's way more than we thought," Jeff said. "Things must be moving fast."

Tiffany nodded. "And the nurse said that the oldest person admitted was sixty-five. That doesn't seem like it's tied to the game, to me."

Mr. Hofstrom stroked his chin. "Well, old folks can play video games, too. But, that raises the question, doesn't it? Are all of them tied to Excalibur? Or is there something else causing it?"

"What else could be causing it?" Jeff asked.

No one had an answer.

"So, how do we stop this vampire queen?" Tiffany asked.

Mr. Hofstrom opened up his Trapper Keeper, the old-fashioned folder where he kept all of his notes on the Otherside monsters. He flipped through a few pages and stopped at a sketch of a dapper-looking man and an elegant woman. Both of them had long hair. He tapped the notebook page.

"This is what vampires look like in their human form. But there are no pictures of their monster forms. Not that I know of, anyway. Also, when I said queen earlier, I should've said king or queen. The person in charge of the vampire hive can present as either a human man or woman. The only way you'll be able to tell is by looking at them in a mirror. You can defeat them by forcing them to look at a reflection of themselves."

"That's it? No garlic, or holy water, or crosses?" Tiffany asked.

"That's it," Mr. Hofstrom said. "You have to be careful, though, because vampires can control their victims like an army. So, if the vampires know what you're trying to do, they'll stop you."

Jeff leaned back in his chair. "OK, but how do we find the creator of the app?" He looked at Mr. Hofstrom and Tiffany.

No one had an answer for that.

CHAPTER TWELVE

Capturing the King

There were fewer kids at school on Friday, and the small number of people left couldn't stop talking about the mysterious ailment that had left most of Devils' Pass Middle School angry and combative.

"My sister said that it's happening at the high school as well," Tiffany said. She and Jeff were a couple of the few kids sitting in the cafeteria at lunch. Most of the other kids hadn't been to school in nearly two days, the day they'd visited Mr. Hofstrom at the library and found out about the vampires.

Zach had stayed home yesterday. Today, Evie was out too.

"When my mom called the doctor, he said as long as Evie didn't have a fever to just let her be. But every time my mom opens her bedroom door to talk to her, she growls and throws things. How can anyone think this is normal?" Jeff asked.

"This goes beyond goldfish memory. These vampires are way more powerful than anything else we've faced before," Tiffany said.

Jeff pushed his food around on his tray. Today was some kind of tuna casserole. He didn't have the appetite to eat anything. He was too worried about his sister.

He needed to find a way to save her from the vampires, but he didn't even know how to find them. And tomorrow he was supposed to dress up as a king for the Excalibur and Nosferatu launch. Everything was a mess, and he had no idea how to fix it.

There was a crash and a scream from the other end of the cafeteria, and a lunch tray fell to the ground as another person went rage case. Abbie Bennett. She stood on a table, kicking everyone else's trays to the floor. The teachers were used to this by now, and they moved in to subdue her without a word.

"Maybe we're going about this the wrong way," Tiffany said. Her tray was still full, and that worried Jeff as much as watching the teachers carry Abbie out of the cafeteria. Tiffany never missed a meal. If she wasn't eating, it meant that she was as worried as Jeff.

"How so?" he asked.

"Maybe instead of trying to figure out who created the app, which we've already failed to do, we should be trying to find one of the other vampires." She tapped her chin as she thought.

"How do we do that?" Jeff set his fork down.

"With a mirror! If we can find one of the other vampires,we can follow them back to the queen or king vampire, the one who created the app. They have to be communicating. And if they're sucking up all this energy from Devils' Pass they have to be close by." Tiffany grinned triumphantly.

"So, we just start looking at everyone in a mirror?" Jeff asked.

She shrugged. "It can't hurt. And the sooner we start, the sooner we can find these vampires and get them out of our town. After all, the vampire is most likely someone we don't know. Otherwise, this would've started much earlier."

"Mr. Vlad," Jeff said.

Tiffany's brows knitted together. "Who?"

"The Nosferatu representative who delivers phones to It's Electric. He's been in town nearly every day since the rage cases started. It has to be him." Jeff slammed his fist down on the table.

Tiffany nodded. "We should definitely get some mirrors and flash him, then. And everyone else in town just to make sure no one else is a secret vampire."

Jeff pushed his tray away. "Yeah, it's time to end this. I don't think anyone is going to miss us. Should we get started right now?"

Tiffany stood up. "Let's do this."

CHAPTER THIRTEEN
Dust to Dust

It was easy to leave school since most everyone had gone rage case, even a few of the teachers. Tiffany led to the way to the pharmacy, where the single clerk looked harried and didn't even notice that the two of them should have been in school instead of buying mirrored compacts.

"That's five seventy-six," the clerk said. Tiffany dug a handful of bills out of her pocket and paid the clerk.

She took her change and grabbed the bag, and they made their way out of the store.

"Sorry, saving for a phone. I'll pay you back," Jeff said, smiling.

"Uh-huh," Tiffany replied, handing Jeff one of the compacts. "Let's just start looking at people and see if any of them are vampires."

"How can we even tell if they are?" Jeff asked.

Tiffany shrugged. "Mr. Hofstrom said if they look in a mirror, it destroys them, right? So . . . I guess we can tell if they are destroyed. Let's split up and make our way down Main Street."

Jeff nodded. He walked toward the diner and It's Electric while Tiffany walked toward the vacuum and sewing machine repair shop. The Yarn and Craft shop were dead, and the bakery was closed, so Jeff wondered if maybe those folks had been afflicted by the Excalibur app as well.

Because he had to be at It's Electric after school, Jeff decided to try his luck in the diner first. He walked in, but as he stood in the doorway, he realized he had no idea how to flash the mirror at folks without looking suspicious. Mr. Hofstrom had said that if the vampires knew people were looking for them, they could turn all of their victims into followers. That was the last thing he wanted to happen.

Jeff stood in the doorway, opening and closing his compact for a moment before he decided to just go for it. He opened the compact and turned around, his back to the room. That way he could see the whole diner behind him reflected back into the mirror.

Everyone looked normal. There was Ms. Joanne, the waitress, and her husband, Mr. Tony, behind the counter. Their son, Evan, worked the grill and chatted with someone Jeff didn't recognize. But all of the people looked totally normal.

All except for the thing sitting in the back booth.

The person there wasn't really a person. It was person shaped, but where its eyes should be were just gaping holes, dark and empty. Four long canines, pointed and white, stuck out of its lipless mouth, and

even though it wore a suit, the gray-green color of its skin marked it as most definitely not human.

There was a vampire sitting in the Devils' Pass Diner.

Jeff froze. He quickly lowered the mirror and turned around. Sitting in the booth, reading a newspaper and looking completely normal, was Mr. Vlad.

Jeff had been right. Mr. Vlad was the vampire king. On his first try, not only had he found a vampire, but he'd found the king.

Jeff's heart began to pound. He wanted to run out of the diner and find Tiffany so she could help him get rid of the vampires. But he didn't want to let Mr. Vlad out of his sight. It was now or never.

Jeff hitched his backpack higher on his back and began to make his way through the diner. As he walked he tried to think calming thoughts, but they weren't very effective. His palms were sweaty, and his leg in the prosthesis was beginning to ache. But he had to do this.

Zach and Evie and everyone else in town were counting on him, even if they didn't know it yet.

Mr. Vlad still wore his sunglasses, and his pale skin looked completely normal. Sun streamed in through the window, but he didn't seem especially concerned. Mr. Hofstrom had said that garlic and holy water didn't work for vampires, and apparently sunshine didn't work, either.

"Jeff! How are you?" Mr. Vlad grinned at Jeff as he approached the table. He looked just like any other adult. Jeff had to remind himself that under the grin was a hideous monster sucking up the energy of his friends and family.

"Good. Uh, Mr. Vlad, I, uh, have a question," he said.

Mr. Vlad folded up his newspaper and nodded. "Sure, Jeff, what is it?"

Without another word, Jeff pulled the compact out of his pocket and held it in front of Mr. Vlad's face. He screamed, and his human appearance melted away, revealing the ghastly gray-skinned, hollow-eyed monster beneath. He then burst into blue flames and disappeared. When the fire cleared, nothing remained of Mr. Vlad but his sunglasses and a thin dusting of gray dirt.

The whole thing took less than a heartbeat.

Jeff began to shake, and he sank down into a chair at a nearby table. Mr. Vlad's newspaper fluttered once and then stilled. Other than that, it was as though nothing had happened.

"Hey, Jeffie, did you want to order something, kiddo?"

Ms. Joanne smiled down at Jeff, and he shook his head. He expected her to ask about the vampire that had just combusted in her back corner booth, but she didn't seem the least bit concerned about anything. She looked at the booth where Mr. Vlad had been and frowned. "I can't believe that guy left without paying for his coffee," she said, wiping off the dirt that had just a few seconds before been Mr. Vlad.

Jeff shifted in his chair, and tried not think of the fact that Ms. Joanne was cleaning up vampire. Or that Ms. Joanne didn't seem to remember anything at all. Goldfish memory was nothing new to Jeff, but it still surprised him every time it happened. He collected himself and then asked, "Uh, I was just wondering if you'd seen my friends today?"

"I saw Tiffany walk by outside a moment ago, but other than that, we've been dead. I did see Mr. Ogilvie this morning and he said you're going to be dressing up for his launch of the new Nosferatu phones tomorrow! I can't tell you how excited I am to get a new phone. Those Nosferatus are so amazing, and they all come with that Excalibur app I've been hearing so much about…" Ms. Joanne kept talking, but Jeff wasn't listening. Instead he was thinking about the fact that he'd just destroyed a vampire. THE vampire, in fact.

Jeffrey the Vampire Slayer.

It sounded ridiculous.

"Thank you, Ms. Joanne, but I have to get to work. I'll see you later!" Jeff climbed out of the chair and made his way outside.

Tiffany was going to freak out when he told her what had just happened.

CHAPTER FOURTEEN

Trust No One

Jeff was so happy when he found Tiffany outside of It's Electric that he couldn't keep the grin off of his face. Sure, he felt kind of bad about poor Mr. Vlad — he'd always been friendly to him — but he'd defeated an actual vampire and saved the whole town. That had to count for something.

"I didn't find anything," Tiffany said, sliding her mirror into her back pocket. "Although the ladies at the yarn shop are having a sale, and there's this awesome purple yarn I'm going to have my grandma get so she can knit me a sweater."

"IkilledavampireohmigodIwassoscared," Jeff said in a rush, and Tiffany's eyes went wide.

"Wait, you found one?" she said.

"I found THE vampire," Jeff practically yelled. "In the diner. The cell phone representative from Nosferatu phones. I looked at him in the mirror and he had these empty black eyes and sharp fangs. Four of them. Anyway, when I showed him the mirror he turned into his monster form and then burned up in blue fire."

"Oh, gross," Tiffany said.

"It wasn't that bad, though. There wasn't anything left behind. Just a little dust and his sunglasses."

"So what did Ms. Joanne say when you burned up a vampire in her diner?"

Jeff shook his head. "She didn't even notice."

"Goldfish memory is a powerful thing," Tiffany said, shaking her head. "Well, this is awesome. I can't believe you did that on your first try! We should check on Zach and Evie now that the vampire king is dead."

"I have to get to work. Mr. Ogilvie is having the Nosferatu phone launch tomorrow and I have to help him get the store ready," Jeff said. His worry about Evie had started to fade as soon as he'd destroyed Mr. Vlad. He was certain she was fine. Now, it was just a matter of getting home and telling her everything that had happened while she was sucked into the game. And, of course, making sure she was no longer focused on Excalibur.

"OK, I'm going to swing by Zach's house and check on him. I'll come by around seven to help you with your costume," Tiffany said.

Jeff made a face and she laughed, and he headed down the road toward the store.

When Jeff got to It's Electric, Mr. Ogilvie was nowhere to be found. But there was a sign on the counter indicating he'd be back later. Jeff went into the back room but he wasn't there. It was strange; it wasn't like Mr. Ogilvie to leave the store unoccupied.

Jeff decided to sweep and take out the trash like
he usually did, and he'd just finished that when the
store phone rang. No one ever called the store, and Jeff
picked up the old fashioned phone under the register
hesitantly.

"It's Electric, uh, Jeff speaking."

"Jeff, it's Tiffany." She was breathless, and it
sounded like she was running, "Zach is full-on rage
case. Growling and angry. I don't think the vampire you
killed was the king. It didn't work."

All of the relief Jeff had felt melted away and a cold
lump of dread took its place. "No, that can't be right.
He had to be the king!"

"I'm on the way to your house right now to check
on Evie. But this is bad, Jeff, really bad. What if we
can't bring them back once they've gone full-on rage
case? What if Zach is lost forever?"

There was a click, and Jeff looked up to see
Mr. Ogilvie looking down at him. "No personal calls
during work hours," he said, and Jeff hung up the

receiver. A chill of fear ran along Jeff's spine, and Mr. Ogilvie pointed to the back room.

"Mr. Vlad seems to be indisposed this afternoon, but we still have to get ready for the sale tomorrow," Mr. Ogilvie said. "We only have a little time, so don't lollygag."

The old man moved to the back of the store and Jeff had a terrifying idea.

What if the vampire king had been someone he'd known his entire life?

What if it was . . . Mr. Ogilvie?

This was Devils' Pass. Anything was possible.

CHAPTER FIFTEEN
Now or Never

When Jeff got home, Tiffany was sitting at the dining room table with his mom, talking about the Fall Harvest dance and how difficult it was to plan a dance in a town where everyone always went missing and monsters were always eating people.

"So far we've had two DJs cancel on us, but to be fair, one was eaten by the dragon that came through last month," Tiffany said.

Ms. Allen laughed. "Dragons! Oh, you kids are so hilarious. I love how rich and fertile your imaginations are," she said. "Hey, sweetie. Tiffany came by to chat with your sister and help you with your costume. I ordered pizza; it should be here shortly. Evie just doesn't seem to be in the mood for company . . ." Ms. Allen's expression turned troubled.

"I'm staying for dinner," Tiffany said, as if there was any doubt. She ate at the Allens' house at least twice a week. Jeff thought she was probably also eating dinner at her own house. At over six feet tall, Tiffany was the tallest girl at Devils' Pass Middle School and definitely the biggest eater.

Once his mom had left the room Jeff sat in one of the dining room chairs and lifted his pant leg to take off his prosthesis. "Why do you always do that?"

"What? Eat at your house? You know pizza is my favorite food," Tiffany said.

"No, talk about all of the monsters and everything with adults. You know they never remember any of it."

"Oh, I know," she said, reaching into her backpack and pulling out a golden cape and gold painted crown.

"But it's kind of like a test, to see if they'll remember anything about what happened. I mean, your mom was swallowed by a dragon and almost digested, and she still thinks the story is just a story. That's amazing. Just how strong is goldfish memory if it can erase trauma? I mean, do you ever wonder why it's happening? Why the adults can't ever remember anything?"

Jeff sighed and removed his prosthesis. "Can we please talk about something else?" He hated to think about his mom getting swallowed by a dragon. It was a bad memory, just like the cancer, and sometimes it was nice to just forget about how scared and helpless he felt back then.

The thoughtful look on Tiffany's face melted away and she bit her lip. "Hey, I'm sorry. Didn't mean to go all science brain on you. Here's the cape and crown I made for you in Life Skills. Good thing everyone's been gone all week. It was easy to get time on the sewing machines. I checked on Evie when I got here — she's still on level sixteen, so we probably have like another day before she goes totally rage-y."

Jeff buried his face in his hands. "I really thought I'd saved everyone when I destroyed Mr. Vlad. I can't believe he wasn't the vampire king."

"So, who do you think it is, then? Mr. Vlad's boss at Nosferatu phones?" Tiffany asked.

Jeff frowned. "No, why do you say that?"

"I looked up the company on the Internet, and there is nothing on any board members or anything. I mean, the name 'Nosferatu' is actually another word for vampire. What if the entire company is nothing but vampires, running a cell phone company from the shadows?" Tiffany said. She pulled out a tube of gold glitter glue and began to drag it along the edges of the crown.

"I didn't think of that. I was thinking it might be Mr. Ogilvie," Jeff said, eyebrows furrowing. He felt a little silly saying it out loud.

"Mr. Ogilvie! But he's lived in town for like forever. Why would he all of a sudden decide to start feeding on the townspeople?"

Jeff shrugged. "I don't know. But when I went in to work today, he was acting weird. And he's the one who started selling the Nosferatu phones in town. Mr. Vlad was in It's Electric almost every day this week. It makes sense that he'd be the vampire king."

Tiffany frowned and set the crown on the table. "I don't know. I guess so. Did you try and flash him with the mirror?"

Jeff shook his head. "I got scared. He walked in and caught me talking on the phone to you and I didn't know what to do after that. I just kind of freaked out, did the rest of my work, and came home."

She nodded. "OK, then our next step has to be how you're going to get the mirror turned on Mr. Ogilvie so we can see if he's the vampire. I have an idea. You still need a sword for your costume, right?" Tiffany grinned like she usually did when she had an especially clever idea.

"Yeah," Jeff said, wondering what Tiffany had in mind.

The doorbell rang and Ms. Allen walked to get it. Jeff leaned in close to Tiffany. "What if Mr. Ogilvie isn't the vampire?"

"Then we're back to square one and Evie will be a full-on rage case soon." Tiffany pressed her lips into a thin line.

Just that moment, Evie walked out of her room. "Hey, guess who just got to level seventeen?" she said. And then added, her voice frustrated and angry, "It's about time." Her hair was greasy and unwashed and there were deep circles under her eyes. She wore the same clothes as she'd been wearing two days ago on Wednesday.

Tiffany's eyes met Jeff's. "I hope you're right about Mr. Ogilvie."

CHAPTER SIXTEEN
The King Is Here

It's Electric opened at ten a.m. the day of the
Nosferatu Extravaganza Sale. Jeff was there at nine
forty-five, bleary eyed and ready to work, but mostly
ready to destroy Mr. Ogilvie.

After a long sleepless night of tossing and turning,
Jeff was convinced Mr. Ogilvie had to be the vampire
king. After all, everyone started going rage-y after the
Nosferatu phones appeared in town. And only folks
with Nosferatu phones could download the app. So, it
all tied back to Mr. Ogilvie.

Jeff arrived wearing his king outfit. He had the crown and the cape Tiffany had made for him with a pair of black pants and a black long-sleeved shirt. He was even wearing his prosthesis, which wasn't nearly as uncomfortable as it had been before. Maybe he was finally getting used to it.

The one thing Jeff didn't have was an idea as to how to get Mr. Ogilvie to look in the mirror. He could just show him his reflection like he had with Mr. Vlad, but it didn't seem like that would work a second time.

"About time you got here," Mr. Ogilvie said when Jeff walked in the door. The pocket mirror weighed heavily in his pocket. He really didn't want Mr. Ogilvie to be the vampire king. He liked the old man a lot, despite his gruffness. After all, he'd let him have a job. He couldn't be all bad.

"Come on, we have a lot to do," Mr. Ogilvie said. The back room was filled with helium balloons and there was a dancing inflatable that had to be put outside and plugged in. But before he could do any of it, Jeff had to see if Mr. Ogilvie was a vampire.

"Hey, Mr. Ogilvie," Jeff said.

"What, kid?"

"Can you take a look at this?" Jeff pulled the mirror from his pocket and held it up to Mr. Ogilvie's face.

Mr. Ogilvie frowned. "Oh, well, why didn't you just tell me I had egg on my chin, kiddo?" He took the mirror and held it up so that he could see his reflection while he scrubbed egg yolk off of his face. "I was in such a hurry to get into the store today, I didn't wash my face. That'll teach me to be in such a rush. Thanks, kid."

Mr. Ogilvie handed Jeff back the mirror and went back to putting the balloons around the store.

Jeff breathed a sigh of relief. Mr. Ogilvie wasn't the vampire king.

Except now, he had no idea who the king was. His heart fell.

All was lost.

Evie was going to lose her mind for sure now.

CHAPTER SEVENTEEN
A Royal Pain

Jeff moved through the next hour in a daze. He stood outside and waved at people when they drove by, and greeted customers as they walked through the door. But none of it really mattered. Soon Evie would fall victim to the time-suck vampires, and he had no idea what to do about it.

"Hey, did it work?" Tiffany asked as she walked up. She carried a foil-wrapped sword, and her sister Simone walked a few steps behind her, her gaze fixed on her phone.

"Nope. You were right. It isn't Mr. Ogilvie," Jeff said. He couldn't keep the crushing disappointment from his voice. He felt like crying.

"Well, that just means we have to figure out who it is, then," she said. "Oh, here, I got this for you." She handed Jeff the sword and he took it.

"Oof, it's heavier than it looks."

"That's because it's magic," Tiffany said, winking.

Jeff looked over Tiffany's shoulder. "Oh, no, is your sister getting sucked into Excalibur, too?"

Tiffany shook her head. "Nah, she's getting sucked into Kevin Donnelly. She's been texting him nonstop for like the last week."

"Don't be jealous because I have a boyfriend and you don't," Simone said. Jeff could understand why boys liked Tiffany's sister. She had the same soft brown skin and her black hair looked like it was made out of clouds. Like Tiffany, she was tall. Unlike Tiffany, she didn't scowl like she was deep in thought. Instead, she wore a wide grin like everything was one big joke.

"Boys find me intimidating," Tiffany said to her sister with an eye roll.

"So get a girlfriend," Simone said, breezing past Jeff and Tiffany and walking into the store.

"Is she getting a new phone?" Jeff asked.

Tiffany nodded. "Yes. So we need to figure out how to stop this vampire nest. Because things are just going to get worse."

A limo pulled up in front of It's Electric, and Jeff and Tiffany both turned to watch as the driver hurried around to open the back door. A beautiful woman with pale skin and long dark hair climbed out. She wore a floor-length dress covered in green and silver sequins and when she moved Jeff was powerless to do anything but watch her.

"Hey," Tiffany said, shaking Jeff.

"Uh, what?" he said.

"I said, 'I wonder who that is,' and you got all spacey and weird and said, 'so pretty.' Are you OK? What just happened?" she asked.

"Yeah, I don't know who she is. We should go find out," Jeff said.

Just then, a group of people shambled up the street toward the store, their steps heavy and slow. Jeff turned toward the sound of the footsteps and froze.

"Tiffany," he said, his voice choked. "Is that Mason Briggs?"

Tiffany paused, her hand on the door handle. "Oh, man, it is. I thought he was still in the hospital from when he got hit by the car."

Jeff pointed to the gown Mason wore. "Looks like he left the hospital and came straight here."

"Look," Tiffany said, her voice getting quiet. "There are Zach and Evie."

There, toward the front of the pack, were Jeff's sister and one of his best friends. They didn't look normal anymore. They looked . . . angry.

Tiffany and Jeff looked at each other as realization dawned.

"Those are totally the queen's followers," Jeff said.

Tiffany nodded. "We need to figure out if the lady that made you all weird is the one. If not, someone else in that store is," she said.

Jeff and Tiffany walked into It's Electric, trying to look normal and not at all freaked out. Everyone stared at the center of the room and the woman standing there.

Mr. Ogilvie, cleared his throat. "Everyone, what an incredible surprise to have such an amazing woman attend our launch here today. Please, let me introduce you all to Katelyn Vestra, the designer of Excalibur, the hottest game around."

Tiffany grabbed Jeff's arm, nearly upsetting his balance. "Jeff," she whispered. "She's definitely the vampire queen!"

Jeff nodded. "And if we don't get rid of her before those rage cases arrive, we are going to have a really messy situation on our hands."

CHAPTER EIGHTEEN

Mirror, Mirror

Jeff looked at Tiffany. "You block the door so that the rage cases can't get in. I'll take care of the queen."

Tiffany squeezed Jeff's arm. "Be careful. And if you need to, use the sword. There's a surprise under the tin foil."

Tiffany nodded and moved through the crowd of people to the door. Most of the people were staring at Katelyn Vestra like she was the most amazing thing they'd ever seen. Mr. Hofstrom hadn't told them that just looking at one of the vampires was enough to put people under its spell.

Jeff sidled up to Katelyn Vestra. There was a woman in front of him, telling Katelyn how much she loved some fashion app. She was saying something and Katelyn Vestra was watching her with a bored expression, but when the woman held up her phone to show Ms. Vestra her app, everything changed.

The phone was in a mirrored case, and the effect on Katelyn Vestra was instantaneous. The vampire took a stumbling step back and screamed. Suddenly, everyone in the room holding a Nosferatu phone screamed with her, their eyes black and empty.

"Jeff, now!" Tiffany yelled. "Use the sword!" She held the door to the store closed, but on the other side all the rage cases battered it, trying to get in. They pounded on the door, their growls loud and clear. Jeff caught a glimpse of Zach and Evie through the glass, and he knew he didn't have much time.

"You think to destroy me?" the vampire queen screeched.

Tiffany pushed the door with all her might, but Jeff could see she was losing the battle. "Jeff! The sword!" she yelled.

Jeff didn't think. He ran toward the vampire queen, the sword with the tinfoil on it held high in one hand.

The woman looked at him and laughed. "You're going to vanquish me with a fake sword, little king?" she said. She grabbed the tip of it and wiggled it back and forth, but it was just what Jeff needed to see what Tiffany had been talking about. The surprise on the sword was a line of tiny mirrors underneath the cheap-looking foil.

Jeff pulled the foil from the sword, revealing the mirrors. He widened his stance to keep his balance and raised the sword up in front of the queen. Light danced off the mirrors.

"No!" the vampire queen screamed. Her beautiful human face melted away. Her eyes were huge, empty sockets with a glowing green speck of light in the middle. Her skin was gray-green and wrinkled like an

old tomato, and her fangs were at least six inches long and dripped with saliva. She reached up to her face with gnarled fingers that were too long to be human and had a couple of extra joints.

"Oh, gross!" Tiffany yelled.

Jeff agreed.

The vampire queen batted the sword from Jeff's hands, and the thing went skidding across the floor, landing under a display of brand new Nosferatu phones. Jeff gasped and tried to dive after it, but the vampire grabbed his cloak, hauling him backward.

"Not so fast," she said, her voice hissing like a snake. Jeff twisted in his cloak, leaning away from the vampire's grip, the cloak cutting into his neck. But then fear froze him when the rest of the people in the store turned toward both him and the vampire queen. Everyone's eyes glowed red, making them look especially evil. They were completely under the vampire queen's spell.

"You will be my extra special servant," the vampire

queen said. Jeff squeezed his eyes closed and tried to think, still leaning away from the queen. He needed a mirror, quick.

In a quick burst of energy, Jeff moved toward the queen so that the cloak had slack in it. Before she could react, he untied his cloak and threw it at her. At the same time, Jeff dropped to his knees. Crawling as fast as he could, he moved past the regular people under the vampire queen's spell and raced toward the display of Nosferatu phones. He could feel the queen's followers starting to grab at him.

"Jeff, hurry!" Tiffany screamed. Jeff glanced back and saw that a few of the queen's followers were trying to yank Tiffany away from the door. If they succeeded, an entire town of people under the vampire queen's spell would be rushing into the store.

He didn't have much time.

He saw a glint of light under the display and lunged. A hand grabbed Jeff's leg just as he latched on to the hilt of the mirror sword. As he was pulled backward, he swung the sword up in front of his eyes.

"No!" screamed the vampire queen and threw her arms up in front of her face. But this time, she wasn't quick enough to avoid the mirror's deadly power. The vampire queen screamed one last time and burst into blue flame as bright as a spotlight.

Jeff hid his face, and when he looked at the spot where the vampire queen had been, there was nothing but a layer of thick dust and a pretty bracelet made of green and blue stones. Jeff reached over to pick the bracelet up, but at his touch, it too crumpled into dust.

He climbed to his feet. All around the store, people were waking from the vampire queen's spell, holding their heads and blinking in confusion.

"I think maybe we should get out of here," Jeff said to Tiffany, who was leaned up against the door, her face shiny with sweat. Suddenly, an uneasy feeling had come over him.

Just as he spoke, every single phone inside of the store sparked, popped, and began to smoke. Mr. Ogilvie looked at the phones and pointed to the door.

"Get out, everyone, get out. Fire, fire!" he yelled.

Tiffany opened the door and people rushed out of the store, a few tripping on their way out. Jeff stopped to help Tiffany's sister Simone to her feet before rushing out of the door himself. Tiffany held the door open for everyone, waving them out of the store. Jeff waited until everyone was out and made sure Tiffany got out too.

Outside, across the street from It's Electric, the crowd watched as the store went up in flames. The people from the stores up and down the street came out and joined them, staring at the fire in wonder. By the time the fire department arrived, there wasn't much of the electronics store left.

"Wow, that escalated quickly," Tiffany said, crossing her arms and shaking her head.

Jeff started to laugh, all of the fear and dread he'd carried around since the beginning of the week melting away. People scattered out along Main Street to watch as the store burned, and Jeff noticed that the rage cases, including Zach and Evie, had all collapsed on the curb not too far away. Everyone looked tired, and more than a little confused, but safe.

He was still laughing when the firefighters finally put out the fire.

CHAPTER NINETEEN
Flipping Out Is Fine

The firefighters had just finished putting out the flames when Zach and Evie finally got up off the curb and walked over to Tiffany and Jeff.

"Hey," Zach said. "What happened?"

"You guys are OK!" Jeff said, high fiving Zach and hugging his sister.

"Yeah. My phone is fried, though," Evie said with a face. "What did we miss? I don't even know how I got here."

Jeff and Tiffany quickly filled Zach and Evie in on everything that had happened since they started playing Excalibur.

"Ohmigod, I threw your tray?" Evie squeaked, looking at Tiffany. "I am so sorry!"

"You weren't yourself," Tiffany said with a shrug. "I mean, you haven't taken a bath for like three days."

"Eww," Evie said, looking embarrassed. She sniffed her shirt and made another face.

"Well, I'm done with phone apps," Zach said. "I mean, my phone is totally scorched, anyway, but if it wasn't, I'd still be finished with phone apps."

Jeff looked past his friends and saw Mr. Ogilvie standing off a little to himself. "Hey, I'm going to go talk to Mr. Ogilvie."

"Oh, poor Mr. Ogilvie," Evie said. "His store is totally ruined."

"We'll meet you at the diner for celebratory milkshakes," Tiffany said, and Jeff nodded and moved toward his now-former boss.

"Hey, Mr. Ogilvie," Jeff said. "Sorry your store is ruined."

"Jeff! Eh, it's OK, kiddo. I was thinking about retiring, anyway. This is probably a sign. My daughter in Florida is about to give birth to my first grandkid, and I think it's probably time to move somewhere warmer. But I'm glad I saw you, though. I have something for you." Mr. Ogilvie walked over to his car and opened the trunk. He came back with a box and handed it to Jeff. "I know it isn't the brand new Nosferatu that you'd had your eye on, but it's still a phone."

The box held a flip phone like the kind Tiffany had. It was a cheap phone and he wouldn't be able to download any apps onto it. But for Jeff at that very moment, it was perfect.

"Thanks, Mr. Ogilvie," Jeff said. "This will work just fine."

Jeff smiled, turned smoothly on his leg with the prosthesis — for once not feeling like it was too small — and walked to the diner to have a milkshake with his friends.

VAMPIRES

Origin: *Otherside*

Colors: *appear as beautiful humans, but when revealed in a mirror, are hideous monsters*

Likes: *all types of energy--physical, emotional, mental. Love creating situations that allow for continuous feeding*

Dislikes: *mirrors; free thought; disobedience; smart humans*

Note: minions will attack when trapped

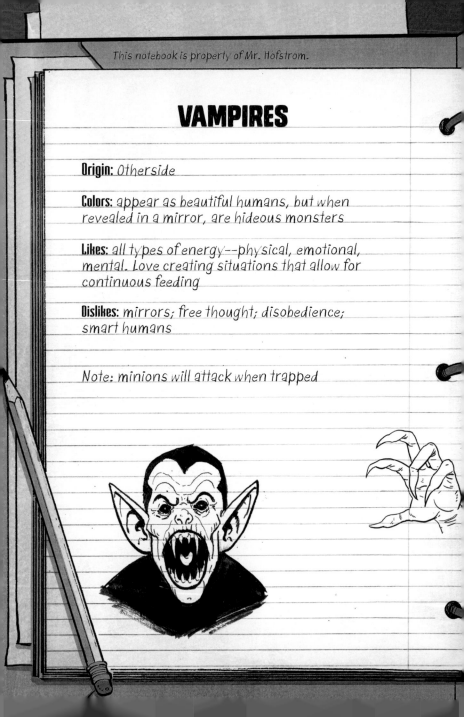

Creatures that feed on human emotions rather than blood, vampires often appear as beautiful men and women with an amazing sense of fashion. They feed on their human victims as well as controlling their minds. The vampires can control any human it has fed from, no matter how recent the feeding. Vampires have a hive mentality, in that lesser vampires work for a lead vampire known as a king or queen. The only proven way to see a vampire's true form or destroy them is with a mirror. By forcing a vampire to look into the mirror they are forced to realize that they are truly a monster and will spontaneously combust.

Note: some vampires have taken to using modern technology to hunt their victims. Watch for addiction to TV shows, phone applications, and online games to find the victims of vampires. The only way to cure the victims is to destroy the king or queen.

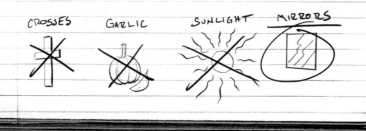

CROSSES   GARLIC   SUNLIGHT   MIRRORS

GLOSSARY

albatross–a type of bird; from the poem, "The Rime of the Ancient Mariner" by Samuel Taylor Coleridge

brandishing–to wave a weapon in threat

corduroy–a type of fabric with raised ridges

hypnotize–to put someone in a trance

intently–with pure focus

intimidate–to make someone feel scared or threatened

lunatic–someone who is not thinking clearly

ominous–scary or creepy

oncologist–a doctor who treats cancer

pacifist–a person dedicated to peace

scowl–to furrow eyebrows in a way that signals anger or displeasure

sedate–to make someone drowsy or sleepy, usually from a medication

sneeze guard–a plastic roof over food at buffets or lunch lines

stocking–to put things on shelves

tendril–usually a long, thin, plant-leaf that reaches out

warranty–a written guarantee

YOU SHOULD TALK

1. Jeff thought the vampire king might have been Mr. Ogilvie. What made him come to that conclusion? Find support in the text.

2. What was Jeff's first clue that the Excalibur game was trouble?

3. Jeff's parents think he is irresponsible with his phones – even though they get damaged while he's fighting monsters. Have people ever misunderstood your actions? Or have not known the full story?

WRITE ON

1. Pretend you are Jeff writing to Mr. Ogilvie and asking for a job. Write down some of the characteristics that make Jeff a good candidate. Now write the email to Mr. Ogilvie.

2. Do you have a favorite game you've played? Write about the game and what made you like it so much.

3. Imagine you are Evie and you want to write an apology to Tiffany. Write an email from her to Tiffany explaining how you were feeling in the moment you acted out.

ABOUT THE AUTHOR

Justina Ireland lives with her husband, kid, and dog in Pennsylvania. She is the author of *Vengeance Bound* and *Promise of Shadows*, both from Simon and Schuster Books for Young Readers. Her forthcoming young adult book *Dread Nation* will be available in 2018 from HarperCollins and her adult debut *The Never and the Now* will be available from Tor/Macmillan. You can find Justina on Twitter as @justinaireland or visit her website, justinaireland.com.

ABOUT THE ILLUSTRATOR

Tyler Champion is a freelance illustrator and designer. He grew up in Kentucky before moving to New Jersey to develop his passion at The Joe Kubert School of Cartoon and Graphic Art. After graduating in 2010 he headed back south to Nashville, Tennessee, where he currently resides with his girlfriend and soon to be first kiddo. He has produced work for magazines, comics, design companies, and now children's books; including work for Sony Music, F(r)iction magazine, Paradigm Games, and Tell-A-Graphics. You can see more of his work at tylerchampionart.com.